INK STAINED LOVE

INK STAINED LOVE

DESIRE AND HEARTACHE PENNED IN POETRY

ERNEST FEDERSPIEL

DEDICATIONS

Ephesians 5:20 Always giving thanks to God the Father for everything, in the name of our Lord Jesus Christ.

Dorothy Jones whose strength, love, and patience were gifts she shared unselfishly throughout her life. She was an angel who walked among us, sharing love and peace. She also showed me the talent of many things lying inside my mind, and it was my choice to open them. *"Rest in peace, dear mother"*.

Ronald "Dawg" Johnston, A lifelong brother, friend, and mentor who shared life's ups and downs with me in this fantastic journey. " *A connoisseur in the growth and caring of marijuana plants and genetics, Rest in peace brother"*.

To my fellow Bloggers on WordPress, Your support and encouragement of my work have given me untold strength and made all this possible. Without your undying support and loyalty, I would have never thought this stage of life could ever come to fruition.

"I offer all of you my complete gratitude and respect".

EPIGRAPH

'Love can sometimes be magic. But magic can sometimes... just be an illusion.' – Javan

INTRODUCTION

Welcome dear readers to Ink Stained Love

My debut book, Ink Stained Love, is a journey through the multitude of emotions that define love. From the first flutter of infatuation to the aching void of loss, these poems are a window into my soul. They are not just words on a page, but whispers of the heart, resonating with anyone who has ever dared to love deeply.

"In chambers of the heart where desires flow with the blood of yesterday and dreams of tomorrow, this book finds its origins. Ink Stained Love explores the depths of joy and the fervor of love's passions, stitched with the threads of my life's experiences."

Each heartbeat whispers of longing, and each pulse testifies to the love that binds us. In this realm of passion and prose, we are entwined in a delicate dance of vulnerability and strength, where every word penned reaches the soul's deepest yearnings.

Welcome, dear reader, to Ink Stained Love, where words are both the journey and the destination.

Ernest Federspiel

ACKNOWLEGDEMENTS

Dawn Pisturino,
Author, *"Ariel's Song"*, *Lunar Gazing Haiku*
Whose words of encouragement and guidance helped me to open up and share my thoughts and words with the world. "Thank you so much Dawn, you'll always have my undying gratitude."

Willie Torrance Jr.,
Author, *The Latter Times of Being Crazy for Christ*, *Take Me Out With The Crowd*
Your mentorship has not only enriched my professional journey but has also profoundly impacted my personal growth. The lessons you have imparted and the insights you have shared will forever resonate with me. "Thank you for believing in me, for challenging me, and for being a constant source of guidance in this process."

For publishing my work on their sites.
Dagmara K. @ SpillWords.com
Kathy Keith @ Medusa'a Kitchen.blogspot.com
Barbra Leonhard @ MasticadoresUSA.wordpress.com

Formatting design, images, and back cover by Canva Pro

Front cover images by Copilot AI designer

With deepest gratitude, Ernest Federspiel

INK STAINED LOVE

DESIRE AND HEARTACHE PENNED IN POETRY

ERNEST FEDERSPIEL

FIRST EDITION

All rights reserved. No part of this book may be reproduced, distributed, or transmitted in any form or by any means, including photocopying, recording, or other electronic or mechanical methods, without the prior written permission of the publisher, except in the case of brief quotations embodied in critical reviews and certain other noncommercial uses permitted by copyright law.

The author owns all rights to previously published poems. They were published under non-exclusive rights [rights revert back to author upon publication].

Disclaimer: The poetry inside reflects the author's personal experiences with love and faith. All poems within this book are creative interpretations of reality, as seen through the author's unique perspective. This book aims to inspire, provoke thought, and provide a sanctuary for reflection. It is not intended to serve as a source of literal fact.

ISBN 9798991383301

Peaceful Insanity Press

copywrite 2024© property of Ernest Federspiel

TABLE OF CONTENTS

DEDICATIONS	I
EPIGRAPH	II
INTRODUCTION	III
ACKNOWLEDGEMENTS	IV
LEGAL PAGE	V
TOC	VI-VIII
INK STAINED LOVE	**1-105**
EPILOGUE	IX
ABOUT THE AUTHOR	X
NEXT UP	XI

---♡---

I'VE SEEN STARS	1-2
THANK YOU	3
HEARTFELT	4
BEHIND A CLOUD	5
CONFUSED RELIEF	6
COME TO BELIEVE	7
WINGS OF ANGELS I	8
WINGS OF ANGELS II	9
FRESH AGAIN	10
TO THE LADIES	11-12
MY HEART SWELLS	13
"LOVE UNTAMED"	14
A CHURCH ON KENTUCKY AV.	15-16
LITTLE CUPID	17
WITHOUT THE WORRY	18
NIGHTTIME JUILET	19-20
MIND & INK	21
SILENT SENTENCES	22
WHAT ELSE CAN I DO	23
WINGS OF ANGELS III	24
COME SUNRISE	25
SOMEWHERE OUT THERE	26

TABLE OF CONTENTS

GOOD-BYE TO THE NIGHT	27
"TEARS FLOW"	28
MELT AWAY	29
MARY JANE	30
A DIFFERENT PIECE OF MIND	31-32
A PRICE TO PAY	33
HELP ME SEE	34
LOOKING STRAIGHT AT YOU	35-36
"WHAT I FEAR"	37-38
GOODBYES	39
THE ONLY REPLY	40
RESERVATIONS	41-42
THE PRICE I MUST PAY	43
DEAR MOM	44
'REMEMBER'	45
REMEMBER WHEN	46
OPEN ARMS	47
AS ONE	48
SINCE YOU'VE KNOWN ME	49
A ELF'S NOTE	50
SEARCHING	51
LONESOME BOUND	52
FULL MOON SIN	53-54
SOUTHERN FLOWER	55
LET ME	56
I NOTICED YOU	57-58
ONE WAY LOVE	59-60
FAST MONEY	61-62
TIGHT AND SLOW	63
MAMA'S POEM	64
DANCE OF ROMANCE	65-66
THE REAL McCOY	67-68
MYSTICAL PHYSICAL	69-70

TABLE OF CONTENTS

WAKE UP CALL	71-72
TOTAL MISTAKE	73
BROWN BOTTLE BLUES	74
I DIDN'T UNDERSTAND	75-76
THE DOOP - DE - DOOBIE SONG	77-78
THINKING	79
"YOU WATCHED ME DIE"	80
FEELINGS I HIDE	81
'AIN'T IT FUN'	82
"WHERE ARE YOU"	83-84
ONE MORE ROUND	85
YOU HAVE BEEN HERE BEFORE	86-88
MY TURN TODAY	89
DREAMS OF YOU	90
TEMPTATION	91
LITTLE SEXY	92
UNBRAVE BRAVE	93
MAGICAL FLOWER POWER	94
STEP INTO THE DARKNESS	95-96
DOUBLE DOWN	97-98
FADE AWAY	99
"TWO MULES"	100
BAD ASS ALICE	101
RUNNING FOR MY LIFE	102
TOLD BY ME	103-104
'THE FINAL REEL'	105
ABOUT THE AUTHOR	IX
COMING SOON	X
EPILOGUE	XI

INK STAINED LOVE

I'VE SEEN STARS

Here I am in my hometown and my back is against the wall
I'm praying to you Jesus, Please help me to see
I've no friends to help me now, I'm losing my sanity
Who am I... supposed to be?

I've run up and down these roads climbing every hill put before me
The twists and turns, stop and go have really took a toll you see
Broken bones, scars abound and tattoos tell of where I have been
Dear Lord through this all you have been my only true friend

I've seen the same stars as you and we have shared the same pain
We've basked in the same sunshine and have all walked in a summer rain
I've plowed through the snow of a February storm
And thawed these old bones in the bright southern sun

I'VE SEEN STARS

Without you, in my life, the joy has diminished and life is just not that fun
I find myself once again toying with the idea of ending all this with a gun
I have seen the stars shining and know you can comprehend my deepest pains
I no longer know who it is that I am supposed to be
Just that without your love, life is just pure misery
So another night finds me in thought beneath the stars that shine
Praying that pretty soon I can find peace of mind

THANK YOU

Dear Lord, I'm just here to say
Thank you again for helping me find my way
I always seem to stumble and fall flat on my face
When I forget to place you in front of the human race
When things are going well is the time I forget to pray
And thank you dear Lord for another productive day
So, I plead with you to please forgive me of my sins
And to bless me with wisdom for both losses and wins
Please make me a better person every day
And may I always remember dear Lord to walk closer in thy way
Amen

HEARTFELT

When I laid my eyes upon you for the very first time
I saw only sadness, pain, and sorrow on a face that couldn't shine
Listening to the turmoil that your soul is going through
Made me wish there was something that I could do for you

I'm not trained to help like that so I'll write you a poem instead
I want you to know there is a brighter future lying ahead
The Lord never gives us too much to carry, although we have our doubts
Believe this one thing lady, this will turn all about

Your soul will soon start burning bright from inside you again
And your light will shine brighter, this I believe my friend
So keep moving forward, it's rough but you have got to try
Someday looking into the past, you'll no longer feel the need to cry

BEHIND A CLOUD

I know that when you see me
I am the star behind a cloud
And if you were my sunshine
My star could shine so proud

The warmth that you could give me
Would make a garden grow
In the middle of that garden
A rose that is my soul

This rose would surely blossom
With petals of love oh so lush
And stretch out to the sunshine
That it needs so very much

This rose just can not grow
My star will not keep shining
Through these clouds around my soul
Without your loves silver lining

The rain that is now falling
Are the tears on my face
Because this lonely rose is dying
Without your sunshine to embrace

CONFUSED RELIEF

I've never heard you sing and I know you are no movie star
Your nylons are ripped and the makeup needs repaired too
Where are you headed on this fine spring morning
Down to the truck stop to earn a buck before noon

I've seen you looking lost as the sun called it a day
And I watched as you sought some confused relief
No association will be found by you today
Human contact stolen from you by an unnatural thief

The man you love is nothing more than a pimp
Hustling the world and using you for his fame
Your false beliefs keep you in a dream of illusion
As you sell your body by the hour for his gain

The road you walk is not paved with silver or gold
But there is an intersection just up the way
The beaten path you walk has been used since the days of old
Turn right, you can be saved by getting on your knees to pray

COME TO BELIEVE

Learn to believe in Jesus and he will set you free
Your troubles will pass when you start bending your knees
Life is a hard struggle when you attempt to do it alone
So try to accept Jesus in your heart and in your home

Things become clear and soon you come to find
Worries disappear and you now have peace of mind
These are not just words written down for you to see
But truth deep down in my heart that I've come to believe

This wonderful faith came upon me out of the blue
When I got on my knees and asked what I should do
A small feeling of peace came and then went away
When at first on my knees I began to pray

At the time I was not ready to truly believe
But that peaceful feeling again washed over me
At last, I think I might finally be starting to understand
The meaning of the poem "Footprints in the Sand"

WINGS OF ANGELS I

The day started as any other
The sun had yet to rise
I got this fantastic feeling
On bent knees and looking to the sky

I saw an angel
Coming down from the promised land
The words she spoke floated out to me
Making me feel like such a simple man

She said "Ernie, time has gone on forever
With no plan on slowing it down"
Heaven is full of souls
That thought they couldn't come around

Your burdens might seem heavy
Stress and worry bring forth so much grief
Put your faith back in Jesus
He will strengthen all of your beliefs

WINGS OF ANGELS II

When you see an angel, you don't always see their wings
Sometimes even angels are burdened with troublesome things
Halo's don't always sparkle the way you think they should
Their jobs are often soiled trying to keep the human race good

We've all had angels in our presence, but we didn't care to know
When we don't pay attention, dissension strongly grows
To cause grief to angels is a sin that shouldn't be done
God has sent them down to us, each and every one

Today is called 'Fat Tuesday' down in the deep south
Tomorrow is Lent, so let prayers spew out of your mouth
I find myself praying every day, but my prayers are incomplete
What I ask for could hurt others, and that is a selfish feat

Getting back to angels, they know what to do and when
When they have to do wrong, they are forgiven of their sins
Angels produce miracles that are not always crystal clear
So remember in your heart to always hold angels dear

The keepers of the masses, they help us when they can
Yes, now and then they are burdened by the ways of the common man
If you get a chance, help an angel dust off their wings
And try not to bother them with wasted greedy dreams

FRESH AGAIN

If you think my heart is aching
Sweetie, you are wasting your time
And if you think my heart is breaking
Your mind is traveling on a dead-end line

Woman, I have never felt better
The weight has been lifted free
My life is just now starting
Since you're away from me

I hear the robins in the morning
Sunshine feels good on my face
I eagerly embrace the warmness
Of getting back into the human race

The pleasure of passing on a smile
Or of getting a wink in return
Letting people see that I am happy
Is a lesson you will probably never learn

So I say so long to trivial matters
I'm looking up some long-lost friends
I'm dumping all of your drama
And starting fresh again

TO THE LADIES

Let's start by talking about my sweet Mother's love
Living proof there is a Lord high up above
Her passion has always stood up to the test
The lady's a true peach, a cut above the rest

Jan is an angel, watching out for me from high up above
If I took all day I couldn't explain all of the untold love
She was always there to listen to me
May she have peace throughout eternity

Carol has stood tall through all her ups and downs
The love that we share is on solid, firm ground
A peach cobbler will forever make me think of her
The love-binding sister that I hold so dear

Sweet Sandy's smile faded away just too damn fast
In my heart a love for her that will forever last
Robbed in her youth by brain tumors and strokes
She's an angel in heaven watching over you folks

TO THE LADIES

Other women have entered my life and left a sparkle on my soul
What I'm trying to say is something all of you should know
Nothing comes close to a woman's warm gentle love for me
Without these feelings where in the world would I be?

Soothing feelings that go way deep down in my heart
Makes life worth living straight from the start
So here's to the ladies, thank you for making all this worthwhile
The heartfelt warmth that you give me radiates through my smile

MY HEART SWELLS

Every day my heart swells until it feels like it wants to burst
Not being able to hold you in my arms makes it all the worst
Emotional torture is the turmoil I seem to be going through
And I believe emotional abuse is what is happening to you

Six months ago I could never have believed
Loving you would grow enough to make my heart bleed
As I close my eyes to sleep our love becomes so vivid in my dreams
Let me show you woman what our love connection could mean

You keeping this secret and letting my love light shine
Would release the chains on this troubled heart and mind
You are a beautiful goddess with a warm and gentle touch
A lifelong partner that I need to cherish so very much

Something special for two people that could remain so pure
A bond of desire and love growing stronger throughout the years
So take my hand honey, and let's start this journey for two
As you read this today, you'll know I'm confessing my love for you

"LOVE UNTAMED"

Back in the warmth of a love untamed
Feel the cool moonbeams as I whisper your name
Notice your hearts flutter as we listen to the wind
Another revelation of sweet romance begins here

The stars all seem a little dimmer
Compared to the twinkle in your eye
Time seems to run a little slower
As we gaze into the darkened sky

I have so much to tell you
But I remain still as I hold you in my arms
I'll make you one small promise
To bring forth no trouble or harm

Alas, it's one more elusive moment
Way too good to be true
As I awaken to find
Just another lonely dream of you

A CHURCH ON KENTUCKY AV.

As I sat inside a house of worship today, peace was found inside
And there might just be redemption if I let Jesus be my guide
No revelation overcame me as I sat and thought about my past sins
When I heard a voice inside say "Welcome back home again"

Although I didn't know the songs, I praised our Lord just the same
A warm feeling came over me when the pastor eased over and asked me my name
She welcomed me into that house of prayer with a warm and friendly grin
She said that I was always welcomed there no matter what my sins

In the past, I have praised and condemned our precious Lord above
But before this day I never truly accepted his undying love
In my mind, I struggle with forgiveness for my selfish ways
As I believe we all do when trying to justify sinful days

A CHURCH ON KENTUCKY AV.

Most of the time we don't stop to see who we hurt or why we made them cry
Our vanity is in full gear and on that feeling we stay high
When we see what heaven holds in store for us to gain on our dying day
Will it be too late to bend your knees and pray?
When I think back on that church scene, I long to find lost grace from our Lord
I feel the love showering over my sinful heart without hearing a single word.

LITTLE CUPID

It's that time of the year, for cupids' little spin
A day of roses, and chocolates and I love you again
Arrows zinging through the air, sometimes they nearly miss
Lovers everywhere, sharing an intimate kiss

Reservations are hard to get, on this special night
Romance in the heart as we hold each other tight
Passionate embraces are on every mind
This is the one day that love truly does bind

And for those lonely people who are drawn within
This is a day of hope that love will conquer again
So get busy little cupid, and let your love arrows fly
Love is taking over, no need to question why

Just make sure your love aim is true
Do the job you are supposed to do
Make two hearts beat again as one
A Spark of Love shows cupids job was well done

WITHOUT THE WORRY

Starting this day without the worry of fear or pain
Knowing our strong love bonds will always remain
Thoughts of midnight sensations that we so much enjoy
Of all the laughter and fun we just seemingly employ

Waking each morning to hear you whisper in my ear
Leaves me feeling peaceful and contented my dear
The elusive moments of desire that we share within our souls
People watch in amazement as daily our love bond grows

The easiness of life when with your hand in mine
We glide through the trials and tribulations of time
Time is a fortune when we are doing what turns us on
Listening to you recall each day is like hearing a new love song

With these fresh songs constantly repeating a loving verse
After saying I do, I got the best without getting the worst
Enjoying every second of every day with you by my side
Is a pleasure I look forward to and hold onto with a special pride

Your brunette hair with age is starting to go grey
My dear, please don't change it as I like you just this way
Time changes little things in life and often big things to
But it could never change the strong love I feel for you

NIGHTTIME JULIET

Step over into the dark side
Where the light is not so bright
And I will name you Juliet
Because it just sounds so right

I'll serenade you with love songs
I'll give you flowered tattoos
I'll treat you the way
That Romeo is really supposed to

So brush your hair softly
Think thoughts of love so sweet
I'll wait to sing you love songs
About tenderness when again we meet

Over on the dark side
Where my love is waiting for you
I will not only be your Romeo
But your Casanova too

I want to caress your soul with love songs
Massage your body with oils
For only on the dark side Juliet
Can our love truly show

NIGHTTIME JULIET

So close your lovely eyes and drift over
Into the dark side to see what you will get
Give a listen to my love songs
And sweet dreams my Nighttime Juliet

Published at MasticadoresUSA 8/15/2024

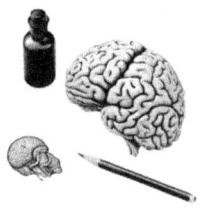

MIND & INK

I give thanks to the Lord high above
He has blessed me with an altered mind and ink
A desire to explore the aspects of love
Mixed with the possibility of making you think

A road often traveled by many before me as well
Words of laughter and sadness mixed in the pot
With the hopes of serenity ringing your bell
And fantasy putting me on the spot

I write these words as they float across the sky
I pluck them out and ink them down
Words that take you on a journey without asking why
Leaving you wanting ...

SILENT SENTENCES

If you'd let me, I could show you such sweet devotion
I write with my eyes, but you don't read the emotion
Silent sentences pour into the air from inside my mind
When you think about me, are your thoughts unkind?

A memory of your past or maybe a bad dream
I'm here to tell you, woman, I am not what you see
Open your heart and read these yearning eyes
You'll find unlimited love, like the stars that fill the sky

If you wanted the moon, that would be ok with me
I'll spend my life giving you cherished memories
Let's build a fire baby, it can start small and slow
With that winking ember, a love universe can grow

Let me whisper sweet nothings into your dainty ear
Help me make this love for you perfectly clear
I'll hold your hand as these flames slowly build inside
Turning into a raging love fire that neither wants to hide

Let's find a tune of shared thoughts in the music of love
I'll shower you with unlimited devotion as I stated above
A fire deep in our souls will make the sun feel pale
Alas, more silent sentences bring another love to no avail

WHAT ELSE CAN I DO

I sit beneath these crying stars
Not knowing what else to do
I have no desire to keep trying
I know I am sure missing you

When the sun starts its daily burning
Rising faster into the eastern sky
I'll hide all of these feelings, and try to be a normal guy

I know inside me that it's useless
As I stumble throughout the day
My thoughts keep returning to you
It's the hard price my weary mind must pay

Soon once again the sun will be setting
Down on the ocean that is so blue
Once again the stars will start crying
As they know I am missing you

Please come home and place yourself in my arms
Or at least get out of my head
I need some peace and understanding
For a love, you think is dead

WINGS OF ANGELS III

After you passed away I saw a new shining star
That's when I realized just where you are
You are an angel, watching over me
Waiting for the day that again we meet

I miss you sister Sandy and your smiling face
Your amazing beauty and astounding grace
So many things I never got to say to you
Since you've been gone my heart has remained blue

A copy of this poem will be placed upon your grave
For another angel working on my soul to save

A DIFFERENT PIECE OF MIND

I found Jesus today, he's been here all along
Peace found in my heart along with a joyous song
I guess I've known this since I was a little child
Not paying attention, I ran free and wild

Feeling I didn't have to pay heed, dues were amassed through time
Paying them all one by one offers me a softer piece of mind
I awake each day with joy in my heart and a prayer on my lips
Before I lay down at night I beg forgiveness for my slips

I have figured out on my own that hell is here and now
I have stopped playing and bend my knees to learn how
Searching inside our souls, heaven awaits to be found
Showing kindness and love puts us on track to the holy ground

PUFF
PUFF
PASS

MARY JANE

Let me spark a flame to this home-rolled
And catch the vapors of Mary Jane
Soon she will set in and a mellow life
Will be tolerable once again

They call it a wake and bake first thing each day
It can bring forth a calmness that lightens up your way
Find the strain that works best for your mind
And catch the vapors of Mary Jane one more time

It works wonders for those who can't eat and others too
If you just want a buzz then this is the plant for you
Unlike cigarettes, this plant will not cause you harm
But rather reduce the stress like a very lucky charm

Mary Jane as it is so often called gives magic relief
No matter what the government wants us to believe
So spark up a bud any way you choose
And let the vapors of Mary Jane chase away those blues

MELT AWAY

Today's dawn brought me a brand new feeling
It's very easy on my soul
Maybe it is because I'm older
And life has brought me a knowledge of control

The beauty that I am seeing is so pleasant to my eyes
The thoughts that I am having should come as no surprise
The Lord has blessed you woman, and now he is blessing me too
As I get such a peaceful feeling when I'm looking at you

Coming or going, or just sitting there in that chair
My heart beats a little faster when I see you there
I long to be with you, and watch your brown hair turn grey
Because each time I look into your eyes...

I simply melt away

"TEARS FLOW"

Your beautiful green eyes showed me
The astounding emotion inside your soul
When standing in your presence
I knew that I was once again whole

Somewhere in time, I'd forgotten
How happy love could make me
The only time I was ever happy
Was when I was hand in hand with thee

Our path has been both smooth and rocky
Ups and downs from the word go
Our love stream ran so deep
And I loved you with all of my soul

Our friendship grew stone cold with age
Thinking of us, emotions stir up into a love rage
As I write down these words of love and hate
I continue to look back, unable to close the gate

So I sit here and write this poem to you
Knowing that it will never be read
And the tears flow freely from my eyes
For a love that you swear is dead

GOOD-BYE TO THE NIGHT

It's five a.m. on April twenty-ninth
The robins are singing goodbye to the night
The sun is on the horizon, trying to break through
Hey pretty woman, I sure am missing you

Life was fun when you were around
But just like you, life has let me down
I'm stuck in a funk, with no direction left to go
And my body's breaking down as I slowly grow old

Making a pot of coffee and lighting a cancer stick
I find myself day-tripping, hoping for another wish
Can't find a job, it's hard to survive without pay
I'd sure like to know why life played out this way

Questions such as these have no answers to be found
I take it day by day, knowing somewhere love still abounds
I won't cry into my coffee, I'm happy to have this day
So sing pretty robins, as I sit here in dismay

Soon the sun will set and we will do all of this again
Sing goodbye to the night, my orange-breasted friends
We will meet again in the morning and I will hear your sweet songs
Laying waste to my sorrows with the coming of a new dawn

SOMEWHERE OUT THERE

Somewhere out there, there is a woman for me
Deep in my heart, I must believe
It's been four and a half years since a lady has been around
And that's a mighty long time for love to be out of town

My mind has gone through depression and insanity
I'm tired of waiting for things that I need
No longer a v-8 hot rod out on the road
More like a back forty mule, carrying a heavy load

Please tell me how to turn this all around
I'm tired of feeling like a sad and empty clown
I need a woman to hold and pour my soul out to
I need a reason for living and to lose all of these blues

My body has been through more than I had planned
But deep down inside, I'm still a good loving man
So lady when you see me, give me an easy-to-see clue
That my love is wanted, and it's wanted for only you

COME SUNRISE

I'm going out to look for something new
Is what I said the day that I left you
I went down to the local watering hole
I was looking for lust and a pot of gold

I laid my hand on a pretty little thing
Whispered in her ear nothing but sweet dreams
She held me close and she held me tight
I thought I had found love on that hot, steamy night

Come sunrise we always clear our heads
It was time to get out of the devil's bed
The song that I heard was Lonely and Blue
Now I'm all alone with nothing to do

Traveling these roads looking for the end
All I find is me starting all over once again
The same old trouble I always seem to find
The problem is, the trouble is in my mind

Come sunrise we always clear our heads
Hoping for better times somewhere up ahead
It's the same old song, lonely and Blue
I choose to live alone, rather than live with you

COME SUNRISE

Someday this long road will come to an end
I'll lie in my grave, reflecting on back when
In the end, we will know no more than this
If you've never felt love, you'll know not what you have missed

A PRICE TO PAY

Been a long long time since this heart has felt such joyous pain
I gave up on the feeling but here comes love again
When Cupid showed up with that famous bow
Wasn't he supposed to shoot someone else also

If he did, where's she? I think he might have missed
These feelings I have flowing in me make me long for a kiss
My desires for you are too strong to explain on this day
When I stop to try, I end up chasing you away

Looking at you, amazing beauty is all that I see
When you're not around, I'm left feeling with an empty need
I want to wrap you in my arms to feel your gentle touch
I want to whisper in your ear how I love you so much

Did Cupid shoot you too but you are not letting me know
Because I fell for you Honey, from your head to your toes
I long to be around you, I dream of us all day through
The list is too long for the things I want to do with you

Candle-lit baths in the middle of the afternoon
Are small things that won't be happening very soon
So I bide my time and hope this love goes away
Rejections and broken hearts are a high price to pay

HELP ME SEE

Where did all of the butterflies go
When in my heart it began to snow
The springtime joys all faded away
When my heart began to turn cold and grey

Was everything destined to remain blue?
Because I was no longer in love with you
How did I let life become so harsh and stale
When did I become so meek and frail

I need the sun to shine back on me
Please show me a clue to help me see
My love for life didn't die
But for the pain, I forgot how to cry

Springtime flowers are what I need to see
The thawing of my heart is what needs to be
Butterflies floating in the air of life
Showing me peace instead of strife

Published on Medusa'a Kitchen 6/3/2024

LOOKING STRAIGHT AT YOU

I know my eyes surely deceive me
As I stroll into the room
I gaze upon your beauty
And my heart goes boom...boom...boom

Something exciting was about to happen
I felt the static in the air
I threw caution into the wind
Because I wanted you then and there

You strolled out onto the dance floor
You had a smooth rhythm in your moves
I was quick to join your rhythmic score
And soon we fell into a lustful groove

We shaked, danced, and rattled
To all of your favorite songs
I knew everything you wanted me to
The foreplay of love being prolonged

You told me that you were single
That you lived with a flair for life
You wanted to live on room service
No way you could be a good wife

LOOKING STRAIGHT AT YOU

You told me you liked to travel
The road was your happy home
I told you not to worry
As I wanted to come along

Years cruising on the road Honey
Time spent in cheap motels
We traveled the roads of the wastelands
And got to know each other so well

Our love was a special thing
A bond that grew so tight
It comes from years in the making
And lover it feels so right

Now I'm sitting in a lawn chair
And still looking straight at you
Even though we are up in age
My heart still goes boom...boom...boom

So granny, let's crank up the music
I'll dance slower with my cane
Let's bump and grind sweetheart
Because you still drive my heart insane

"WHAT I FEAR"

You're off again, running fast
I'm drinking beer trying to forget our past
A long, rough road brought me here
When you're done with me this is what I fear

Heartbreak and pain is what is waiting for me
It's already started and this I can see
You're on my mind both day and night
My heart is breaking and it's a sad, sad sight

I can't say to you what is in my heart
As I already know the fight would start
So as I sit and wait for you to come home
It hurts to know that I'm soon to be alone

Remember the market, I had planned that special day
To capture your heart and melt it away
Now for the most part, I can't handle any more pain
After him, we can never mend this broken love again

Tears stung my eyes as I sat in that damn jail
Giving me the time to think of you and how I failed
My eyes met with yours the day I got out
Your lips locked in and I lost your pout

"WHAT I FEAR"

There is a stubborn streak standing in our way
And these are the dues that both of us must pay
Just to let you know that I still want you here
Is my biggest heartbreak of what it is that I fear

GOODBYES

Honey, sit down beside me, I want you to listen to what I say
I will always care for you, but pride got in the way
I thought I could love you, but I don't have what it takes
When I think of us, it's a toss-up of love and mistakes

Sweetie, you came in this knowing I was a basket case
You tell all your friends your time with me was a total waste
Sometime in the future, our failures will be confirmed
Another love affair up in flames and hearts that were burned

I don't think I will say that I'm sorry, as we both are to blame
I will just say goodbye and that this loss is surely a shame
Goodbye my sweet valentine, I hope your light continues to shine
And you find deserving love to last you a lifetime

THE ONLY REPLY

I've run down these streets now for most of my life
I never bothered man with my worries or strife
Knowing it won't be long before they call my name
I'll stand alone with my head hung down in shame

At those golden gates, I'll have to pay my dues
Then is the time that I will reflect on you
You tow the mark and you walk the line
When the chips are down you just keep on trying

I wander this earth, much like the gypsies do
I don't ask for much, I just breeze on through
The same blood courses through our veins
You found logic while I went peacefully insane

We have had times both thick and thin
I stop to reflect on this now and again
Out in the world, your face is the one I miss the most
And when I raise my glass, it is you that I toast

You stood tall and have earned much respect
I lived under a magnifying glass as a suspect
When Saint Peter asks me what I should have done
I can only reply, "Be like Mama's middle son"

RESERVATIONS

My baby told me she was leaving Saginaw
She had better things to do
Fall was just around the corner last week
When I saw her leaving town with you

I'm spending my days at a bar called Stelly's
I'm drinking my troubles away
I called an old girlfriend just to reminisce
But she wouldn't give me the time of day

Bartender, give me a shot of Jim Beam
Better bring a Pabst's blue ribbon too
I'm making reservations for a brand-new life
On white sands with blue water and bamboo

Got rid of my chaps and bought new sandals
I sold my old Harley too
Cashed in my chips and bought two tickets
I'm going on a Caribbean cruise

There is a lady I knew in my younger days
She holds a special place in my heart
I'm going to call her and see if she's willing
To go and make a brand new start

RESERVATIONS

Hey bartender, make it two more pina' coladas
A dozen on the half shell sounds good too
New reservations with a brand-new life
On these white sands, I no longer feel blue

Hey bartender, she wants an umbrella in her drink
She's wearing that bikini and making me think
I'm ecstatic that she wants me to be her man
As we live out our lives on this beautiful white sand

THE PRICE I MUST PAY

Love, you were around me all of the time
Why couldn't you see what was on my mind
You told me that you loved me and said that you cared
I'm sitting here baby and you are... I don't know where

I should have sensed our love starting to die
But slow to catch on, I can only sit here and cry
I should have sensed our love starting to fade
I didn't catch on until you went away

Now I am lonely and dare not go outside
I don't want to let our friends watch me cry
The sunshine, would hurt me, burning into my blues
I'm sitting here baby, where the hell are you?

The walls remain silent as they listen to my moans
I pray into my pillow for you to come back home
Honey, I miss you and need you oh so bad
I miss you and the love that we once had

I should have felt our love start dying
Slow to catch on, so now I sit here crying
I should have sensed our love going away
I wasn't paying attention and this is the price I pay

DEAR MOM

Your eyes were the first to gaze into mine
Your love would stand tall through the trials of time
You showed me tenderness and taught me simple things
Like how to walk, how to talk and never to be mean

A picture of us on a brick sidewalk that we built when I was small
A memory of something I did that had you standing proud and tall
I was your baby, the last one in our family line
And I'll remain your baby, through the ends of time

I thank you for life lessons, and your kind and gentle heart
For always being there even when we were miles apart
I thank you for the forgiveness when I was caught doing wrong
I want to give you the love that I have neglected for so long

I stopped to smell the roses and what I found was you
And I see your love is richer than any gold or jewels
I want the world to know just how I feel deep down inside
Dear Mother, when I think of you my heart bursts with pride

REMEMBER

When I was young you watched me run and play
As I grew older the neon lights took me away
Our paths were different but crossed now and again
Through it all, you loved me until the end

Years have passed and silver has entered our hair
Believe this Mother, I still love you and care
Every day should be filled with laughter and joy
You'll get help with that from your baby boy

Not everything is going to be ok, try and remain calm
Simple things will scare you and cause you to have false alarms
I'll be there to reassure you and try to help ease the pain
I'll share the joy of the glimpse of your former self now and again

Simple things are no longer simple, fear has now taken their place
But your love for me still brightens your beautiful face
You'll find sweet lady that I will always be right here
To fight for you the battles of confusion and terror
You brought me into this life and helped me to see
Not everything is right or wrong, dementia scares the shit out of me

REMEMBER WHEN

Do you remember back when you called me your friend?
You would stand beside me through thick or thin
All the nights we partied up till the break of a new day
Before the meltdown that forced me to go away

We would love the ladies and fly our patches in the wind
Brother, do you remember the fun we had back then?
The night I played fireman and broke into your room
Waiting for the bullet that would bring me to my doom

The day that I met you I broke down on the road
And here came my out-of-town brothers to ease my heavy load
We rambled and gambled, they called us sinful men
Brother, do you remember why you were my friend?

Thirteen years passed us by before I showed up back in your life
You married a different woman and I no longer had a wife
Let me ask the question, which is the greater sin?
Sitting behind bars or sitting here remembering back when?

I don't ride a bike anymore and now just waste my life
Time took a toll on me and left me guessing why
I hope to get through this and return to the person you knew
Dirty Ernie died and this is making me damn blue

OPEN ARMS

I feel you coming with the breeze of the wind
I open my arms to a long-lost friend
We can let time go by as our minds relax with ease
Let's talk about whatever the hell you please

Peaks and valleys have described our lives
We parted ways because of passionate lies
Years have come and years have gone
Let's not sweat little things that went wrong

My hellcat ways have diminished with older age
Being replaced with manners and grace
No whiskey on the table or beer on my breath
Quit doing the drugs that now scare me half to death

I feel you coming on the breeze of the wind
And I open my arms to welcome you in
God has forgiven me of my wicked and fast past
Through this journey, our friendship found a way to last

Once again our laughter can ring across the land
We can rejoice in the bond of true and trusted friends
I feel you coming with the breeze of the wind
True brother ties are being woven once again

AS ONE

It started bright like the sun breaking into a new dawn
Within hours, it was the start of a relationship getting it on
Two years of friendship was but a blink in the eyes of time
After that, I was yours in heart, soul, and mind

Turbulent waters cascade over the deep long falls
To settle into a pool of calmness where serenity calls
New moons rise and fall teaching us that love can not be bought
You fill my waking moments with strong and pure thoughts

The beauty of the dove gliding forth above the morning dew
Sustains a greater tarnish when compared to my love for you
As the earth slowly rotates around our life-giving sun
I cherish and treasure the precious moment that we became one

SINCE YOU'VE KNOWN ME

Since you've known me I've been single
You've often heard me say that I'll stay that way
Lately, when I look at you I get to feeling tingles
And I act like a puppy who has lost its way

I've had love before and I lost it
Bad times seemed to replace the good
I quit going home to find good lovin'
Started doing things I never have should

I turned my back on those I should have cherished
Bars and Loose Women became my favorite past time
That's when my heart started growing colder
Loneliness started to creep into my confused mind

You showed me a new way to look at love
You have shown me it can be ok
I wake up now and enjoy the sunshine
Knowing I will be with you every day

You have opened my eyes again to love
Showed me that tenderness inside me remains
You filled my soul with happiness replacing the pain
Lovely lady, you have made living worthwhile again

ELF'S NOTE

Here it is Christmas time again, so read this little note
I sitting at the North Pole just freezing my tiny toes
I see Santa pretty close to all of the time
Yes I'm an ELF, and no I'm not losing my mind

Snow on the ground and icicles on the trees
Presents to be wrapped, so be good for me pretty please
Dancer's outside playing and Vixen is out there too
Rudolf's polishing his nose, he is ready to come visit you

The North Pole is abuzz with fresh activity
I have to be finished before Christmas eve
Ms. Claus just got home and wants me to do a run
There is just so much to accomplish it's no longer fun

Coffee to be made, thousands of cookies too
Santa needs the energy to deliver these presents to you
Alas I say goodbye, so long for a little bit
I must get busy, helping Ol' Saint Nick

SEARCHING

Another day floats gently into the past
And I age gratefully into the dusk
Reflecting upon the events and times that have been
I wonder where this soaring bird will land

A tea kettle throws steam as the new day approaches
Sweet smells fill the air like honey on a crisp new sea
Life is already getting better
Somewhere love is searching for me

A leave breaks from its branch and soars slowly away
Winter is upon us and soon the branch will bud anew
Again the days will be long instead of dark
Somewhere love is searching for you

A bubble appears in the ocean soon followed by a few more
New ground breaks on the horizon, an island in the making
New events and new times are coming
Somewhere love is searching for us

LONESOME BOUND

You say that I'm a dreamer
Dreaming my life away
There are things worse than dreaming
Like complaining every day

When I met you, you were so happy
Smiling and joking all of the time
There was never a care or a worry
You went along like everything was fine

Unfeeling love must have hurt you
Your smile turned into a frown
You lost your glorious edge of laughter
Now you're bringing everybody down

Pick your spirits up and do it in a hurry
Wipe off your jeans and don't look back
Please quit all that damn complaining
Because karma doesn't get into that

There is a moral somewhere in this poem
You got stuck with the blues of feeling down
Cheating ways from insecurities of a doubtful mind
Has cost you my trust and now for you it's lonesome bound time

FULL MOON SIN

I pulled into Cherry Valley in my pea-green Ford
Had to get some gas from the quick mart store
A cute little blond staring straight at me
Said "I'll show ya something mister that you ain't never seen"

I paid for my gas and we cruised out of town
Headed up in the Cali mountains where no souls would be found
She told me "Pull up in this path, There's a creek up ahead"
"We can go skinny dipping while we listen to the Grateful Dead"

She jumped out of the truck before it came to a stop
Wiggled and giggled while she pulled off her top
I swear that the water was freezing as we both jumped in
This was the beginning of the Full Moon Sin

We swam for quite a while and later danced under the moon
Come daylight I asked her if she wanted to jump the broom
She dipped down, spun around, and smiled up at me
She said "I can't marry you, sweetie, I'm the Queen of Cherry Valley

FULL MOON SIN

We made love in the back of my truck again and again
I'll never forget the night of the Full Moon Sin
I took her back to the valley and as she left my pea-green Ford

She remarked "I swear to ya Ernie, I could ask for no more"
"You're the best lover that's ever been
And I enjoyed that Full Moon Sin"
This is the tale of the Cherry Valley Queen
The kinkiest little blond I have ever seen

Published at Medusa'a Kitchen 6/10/2024

SOUTHERN FLOWER

When you look at me you have no clue
Sweetheart the feelings I'm feeling for you
It is my heart's strongest desire
To hold you as my southern flower

Every morning I awake and I am all alone
If I had your number I would telephone
The sunlight that you could shine on my soul
Could make this lonely man feel so whole

These feelings of love could have so much power
If only you would become my southern flower
We could go out on a picnic or two
As long as I could spend time with you

So will you please give me just one hour
Let me plant my seed and we can reap the power
Of a magical life filled with hot honest emotion
Please become my southern flower of passionate devotion

LET ME

This poem is way overdue
I need to confess my feelings for you
I'm telling you woman that it is driving me mad
To know deep down you're feeling so sad
I love you

Let me bring you laughter
Let me chase away your pain
I can shower you with love
Over and over again
I need you

Your troubles need to be chased away
In my arms is where you need to stay
Your life has been up and down
I want to help you turn it back around
I love you

Let me bring you joy and fun
Believe me, honey, I am the one
I'll provide you with sweet dreams tonight
And hold you in loving arms so tight
I want you

I NOTICED YOU

As I write these words of lust, as I write these words of love
I compare you with the beautiful goddess Venus from high above
Helen of Troy would worry if in this time she was around
Your sensuous beauty would leave her standing on common ground

I see the spark of compassion when I gaze into your eyes
The Gods sitting high above, at night, hear my lonely cries
Your inner beauty shines brightly when you look at me
My soul cries out to you, but my love you just won't see

I awake every morning, you are the first thought on my mind
Not being able to show you my feelings is considered a major crime
I cherish the elusive moments that alone we get to spend
Not showing my lust and love is a hard game to pretend

Your hair is hanging low, and the beauty of a perfect nose and chin
Feature's so lovely, I can't wait to see you again
I gaze upon your breasts, and how that little tummy turns me on
Those amazing hips are just where my hands belong

I NOTICED YOU

My lust for your slender legs, and those tiny, cute little feet
When I see you from behind, my poor heart skips a beat
Holding your hand so soft and warm inside of mine
To whisper sweet words of love to you all of the time

Going back into history, tragic love stories are to be found
I'm sorry to say this, but another one is being written down
Greek mythology plays out on the stage within my mind
I watch as your beauty shines above all else in space and time

I write these words of love hoping someday that you might see
The lust in my heart, pouring out to you from me
I try to hide these feelings to bring no harm to you
Baby, it is tearing me up inside and leaving me oh-so-blue

ONE WAY LOVE

From a mid-eastern town where my life began
I hit the road with an ounce in my hand
I went out looking for a fortune
Learning what it took to become a man

I searched the California mountains
Found one-way love and not much else
Those years have become memories
Who is there to blame except myself

Baby girl showed me things in Texas
She thought every man should know
And all those long hard lessons
Still pleasure women wherever I go

A trip to Lawrence Kansas
Took me through Fayetteville
I met a razorback woman
Who soon fell under my spell

Met Kentucky Rosie on the Ohio River
A weekend of lust as the boats raced by
I taught her secrets of passion
When I left, I left her satisfied

ONE WAY LOVE

Penicillin Patsy lived on the Maryland coast
She used to love it when I made her curl her toes
My kind of woman, she lived her life in sin
She still floats across my mind now and again

Met Bobbi in New York City
I spun her fast world around
When I left the rotten apple
She swore the best had just left town

Auburn Annie knows that she misses me
And all the raw emotions that we had
When Karen passes over my mind
The thought leaves me feeling so sad

I look back into my past and find
I discovered lust and not much else
One thing that remains beyond and above
The one true constant was only one-way love

FAST MONEY

Run baby run just as fast as you can
Run baby run, straight on back to me
I swear I will buy you that diamond ring
Just hurry on back, you sexy little thing

Put that ring on your finger, chase away those blues
Hurry back baby, you've got nothing to lose
The man you are with doesn't mean a thing
He'll treat you bad, and then he'll treat you mean

So come on lady, what do you say
Come home my love, and do it straight away
Listen to me honey, fast money does not last
If you stay with him, then you can kiss my ass

Your little sister might know a thing or two
So maybe she would like this shiny diamond ring
In my heart, I believe she would be true to me
Because she told me, for me her heart bleeds

She's offering love that is solid and true
She promised devotion, just the opposite of you
I told her I had to give you one more chance
As you will find out, fast money just doesn't last

FAST MONEY

Baby, I guess what I am trying to say
Is that I want to be with you until my dying day
But I won't sit by and waste my life
If I can't have you, I'll make your sister my wife
Please don't come home if you can't remain true
As that would make all three of us blue
Me and little sister will put you into our past
As you learn the lesson, that fast money just doesn't last

TIGHT AND SLOW

I've been called a rockin' roller and been called a bully too
I've always dug my country music the same as I dug you
I have to tell this story before it's time to go
As this is a story, I want the whole world to know

My momma and poppa got together one last time
I was raised on Little Jimmy Dicken's and Miss Patsy Cline
My heart always beat faster, come late on Saturday night
The evening winding down and dancing became slow and tight

Soon I hit my teenage years and country music fell far behind
I found rock and roll, and it truly just blew my mind
Just wanting to take the time to let you know
I want you back in my arms, so we can again dance tight and slow

MAMAS' POEM

Sitting here in Dallas with my wife on my mind
Gonna write her a poem since it's been a long time
We've sat in stormy weather, had picnics in the snow
You're forever on my mind and this you should know

We've drank champagne in the water
Shared wine and cheese on a lake of ice
Drank beer straight from the barrel
And you have completed my life

The war is now over and in its place is peace
Forever in eternity, we can remain at ease
From the day I first met you
This love has run deep and true

Knowing we've stayed together is to know a magical feat
To be in your arms tonight would make me feel so complete
I should be on the road again, but I've got no place to go
I am stuck down here in Texas, under my minds heavy load

DANCE OF ROMANCE

Here we go again, another sweet dream love affair
The time is right and the feelings are ripe
Arrows are flying through the air

You looked my way and batted those emerald-green eyes
They caught me completely off guard
We started the dance of sweet romance,
Finding it was not so hard

I'll chase you and you chase me
Until we meet in the devil's bed
After planting my seed and fulfilling your deepest needs
We will start to clear our heads

Time went by and we are no longer high
On Cupid's little game
A routine starts, we break each other's hearts
Then hang our heads in shame
I'll step out, you'll step aside
And at night your tears will flow

DANCE OF ROMANCE

Realization sets in and we begin
To understand how love affairs go
I go left, you go right and we walk on alone
With battered hearts, we slowly leave
The dance of romance alone

THE REAL MC COY

She said that I wasn't the real McCoy
I was just passing through and that she wasn't a toy
She said "Don't wind me up just to let me down
I'm not that kind of girl, and I don't need you around"

She put her heel in my chest, pushing me back into my chair
Looked me in the eyes and said "Listen here"
"Boys like you are fun to ride,
But you haven't got any heart inside"

And let me tell you one more thing
A girl like me likes shiny things
I want love straight from the heart, nothing less
Now tell me, boy, are you up for the test?

I am not a toy to play with and put down
I want a one-woman man that will stick around
I need a little house with a white picket fence
With kids running around full of mischief

I need money in the bank and a little security
Are you willing to give all that to me?
I told you, I'm not a toy to play with and put down
By some fast-talking man on his way out of town

THE REAL MC COY

I'm the kind of woman you want to settle down with
If that's not what you want, then beat it down the path
Just by looking at you, I see you are not the real McCoy
I need a man and you're just a boy

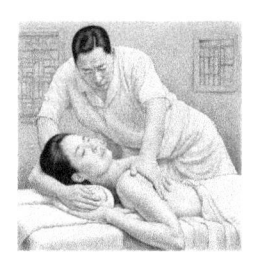

MYSTICAL PHYSICAL

This is a mystical physical, it starts with me rubbing you down
A long-time ritual you enjoy when I pass through your town
Your eyes light up and your skin starts to tingle at the thought
When I ring you and tell you about the chocolates and toys that I have bought

You wipe the calendar free and tell me you are open to new things
You can't wait to see what the nighttime hours will bring
Rose petals leading to a heart-shaped tub filled with bubbles
Tenderness getting ready to ease all your strife and troubles

A glass of fine wine in the hot water produces shimmers galore
Before I even start you are telling me that you want more
I begin with the ankles and the balls of your beautiful feet
As I make my way up to your knees you start to feel the inner heat

The map traced across your skin is tongued in a warm slow motion
Bringing forth moans and the desire for more of this commotion

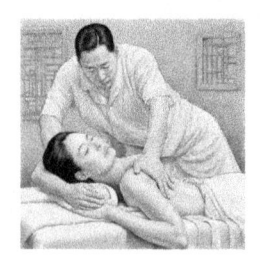

MYSTICAL PHYSICAL

The navel tastes sweet before I roll you over to the other side of bliss
With the cherry oil, your skin warms up to the feel of a slow hot kiss

Love-making sessions that last all night begin to slowly take shape
The multiple ecstasies you experience are chalked up to a pleasurable fate
As the sun rises in the morning you are still in the heat of the night
After complete body satisfaction you know everything is going to be alright

Published on SpillWords.com 8/30/2024

WAKE-UP CALL

I look at you and I wonder why
I give you my money only to hear you lie
I work my fingers down to the bone
Only to call and find out you're not at home

I know you are out running on the town
This bullshit is bringing me down
In your low-neck dress and high-strapped shoes
Honey, you're giving your ol' man the blues

All those guys giving you their best grin
You blow them off and then go back again
Out on the dance floor, shaking what you got
I love you baby, but this has got to stop

When we were young, we were wild and free
But you can't keep acting like you're eighteen
If you don't love me, woman don't come home
Then I could justify being lonely and alone

While you are out chasing another man
I packing my things with a brand new plan
In time you will realize what this is
You've lost the game playing hit-and-miss

WAKE-UP CALL

I'm leaving you now, I'm gonna git up and be gone
I'm searching for true love as I have all along
You will end up old and all alone
I'm stepping away from a street walker without a home

TOTAL MISTAKE

It's a total mistake... baby
The road we will take...maybe
I just want you to see
What you are getting into
When you get into this with me

It's a bright day...baby
It starts this way...maybe
But the clouds soon roll in
And the mistrust begins

Are you getting into this with me?

Soon the warmth turns cold
Our relationship starts to grow old
And you are into this with me

The phone calls will start
You'll come home after dark
Telling me your sister had the flu
Now I'm getting into this with you

Are you sure you want to
Take this love that is brand new
Is it really for you

Or is it a total mistake

BROWN BOTTLE BLUES

I have a picture in my mind of how it's supposed to be
Seems like it never quite worked out that way for me
A lovely little brunette spun my heart around
Lust took over and common sense left town

I lost my job spending time with her
I lost my wife because of the hurt
The kids are all grown, haven't seen them in years
So I drown my troubles in this half-warm beer

I quit going out on the smooth dance floor
Got the brown bottle blues and don't care anymore
Everything I own is sitting on top of this bar
Enough for about two more mason jars

I have a picture in my mind of how it's supposed to be
But it never quite worked out that way for me
Faded memories haunt my mind both night and day
These brown bottles help me keep them at bay

I'm sitting here on this stool, no grin can be seen
Life has me feeling low down and dirty mean
I have to face the fact that I have nothing more to lose
Except my mind to these brown bottles blues

I DIDN'T UNDERSTAND

Came into this world the son of a troubled man
There were many things I didn't understand
I grew up cold and I grew up fast
I found love but it would not last

The highway called out my lonely name
I hit the road to try and ease the pain
Met a woman somewhere out there
She showed me my heart could care

I settled down walking hand in hand
She had me feeling like a complete man
Then I woke up one day to find
She was gone, a memory in my mind

Like a bad dream that haunts my soul
I closed my heart and let love go
My tear ducts have all but ran dry
And for that girl, I no longer cry

As I sit here on this riverbed
Thoughts of death dancing through my head
I know that I'll get up and walk away
Suicide will have to wait for another day

I DIDN'T UNDERSTAND

Came into this world the son of a troubled man
There is still a lot that I don't understand
I grew up fast and I grew up cold
I know that I want to live long enough to grow old

Off the road now, I have settled down
Anger has gone and peace and love have been found
I have sons and brothers that come around
And love has been here all along

THE DOOP-DE-DOOBIE SONG

I woke up from a dream with daylight still far away
I had some time to ponder before I started my day
I looked around the room, the motel was called the Last Stop Bay
Before I left out of that room, this is all I had to say

Doop-De-Doobie, Doobie-Doop- De-Dobbie-Doobie-Doop

I heard a phone ringing, they were looking for triple-A
I told her she had the wrong number, she asked if I wanted to play
We talked for half an hour before she suggested we meet
I jumped on my bike and headed over to Montague Street

I found a place to park and entered the Drunk Patron Bar
I laid eyes on her and knew I had come too far
That woman was lovely with her red hair flowing down
A diamond bracelet on her ankle and lips of dark brown

As I eased up beside her, she asked me what I wanted to drink
Before I could answer she said "Tequila's what I think"
She told the bartender to set up a double round
She walked over to the juke and asked if I could get down

THE DOOP-DE-DOOBIE SONG

I woke up in the morning, I was back at the Last Stop Bay
My head was kind of foggy but I think I heard her say
Doop-De-Doobie, Doobie-Doop, De-Doobie-Doop
By the time I fully awoke, she was gone from the stoop

A hot shower and then I turned in that motel key
Riding out of town her face returned to me
Someone I will always remember, her beauty and grace
That gorgeous red hair and the brown lipstick with the sticky taste

THINKING

He was a legend, a memory in her mind
A projector of a simpler time
The past is never scary
It is the present that holds fear

And the mind keeps thinking...

Thoughts are like flies, here for a moment and then gone
She wished she had him back, to hold back the tears
He had wings like an angel, with a pure demonic grin
He used to say how fun it was being him

And the mind keeps thinking...

He was a memory, could be either good or bad
But that he was a memory is what made her so sad
Her hero of imagination, her knight of days old
The man she loved to remember, always brave and bold

And the mind quits thinking

"YOU WATCHED ME DIE"

I watched me die eight years ago
How she broke my heart no one will ever know
I fell in love way back when
But I fell from grace and now wallow in sin

Does she think of me, I have no clue
Does she dance on my grave, when she talks to you
I watched me die eight years ago
When she slept with you, she killed my soul

I became a drifter, I was lost in the wind
There was no path to return home again
Someday I'll be found in a potters lot
My knowledge of love forever lost and forgot

This life of pain is what she left behind
The pain shot through my heart into my mind
You watched me die as you read this poem
From a shattered heart and broken home

FEELINGS I HIDE

I've put my feelings in check, they will be shown no more
I hide these feelings behind my heart's locked door
There is no reason to feel such heartbreak and shame
So I deal with rejection and conceal all of my pain

Life goes on or so I've been told
This raging fire inside will become ash cold
I'll learn how to become a solitary man
Love has forsaken me once again

The feelings I had for you were never really understood
But when you were around I always felt so good
I enjoyed the smile only you could put on my face
Every time I was blessed to be near your loving grace

These days I turn around when you look my way
Ashamed is a new sensation that seems like it's here to stay
I'm not trying to hurt you, but instead to hide the pain
I've come to understand my love is a loser's game

I make my exit, straight to the closest gate
Hoping you don't see me, can I get out before it's too late?
Because you would say hi and want to chat for a while
And the pain I would feel inside could not be hidden with a smile

'AIN'T IT FUN'

You can rock my world
And bring me glorious pain
I can chase you away
And welcome you back again

You can make me laugh
And you can make me cry
You have me spending all my money
And never questioning why

You can wake me up
In the middle of the night
Telling me things
That makes me feel so right

Ain't it fun being you
Always happy and never blue
It's damn sure fun being me
Waking you up by tickling your feet

"WHERE ARE YOU"

I stood down on the avenue
Head in a fog, I was looking for you
I heard screams from nighttime things
Worry set in for your well-being
Where are you?

A cop cruised by and he was moving slow
Looking for criminals who were looking for blow
Money changing hands in the darkness of night
Words raised in volume followed by a fight
Where are you?

Gunfire screams from up around the bend
I'm worried for you woman once again
I clear my throat and call out your name
Hoping you're not caught up in some deadly game
Where are you?

Nighttime slowly gives way to the rising dawn
I hear no more voices, everyone has gone
Sunlight starts to burn my eyes
And voices inside my head start to cry
Where are you?

"WHERE ARE YOU"

Making my way back to the avenue
I listen close but there is no news
The voices in my head start to fade away
While people with guns continue to play
Where are you?

ONE MORE ROUND

I call your name out in my sleep
I beg the Lord on bended knees
For one more chance to be with you
I'd gladly give up this old barstool

I call your name and not one sound
So bartender if you please, one more round
As I sit here on this worn-out barstool
The juke playing a song we once knew

I remember how we danced every time it played
Life was so sweet before you went away
I scream your name in the middle of the night
What can I do love, to make it all right

Please believe these words that I say
To get you back any price I gladly would pay
I'll keep floating my mind at the bottom of this glass
As I have no future without you and regretfully miss the past

YOU HAVE BEEN HERE BEFORE

You stand alone in the dark chamber, You have been here before
Your mind is racing and so is your heart, as you tally up the score
A smoke-stained barely lit lightbulb swinging, softly in the stale air
Brings back memories of a time when you thought he still cared

Love was supposed to be happy, always leaving you in total surprise
But it never seemed to work out that way, more like cheating and lies
The games start the same way, "Baby I'll be home late tonight"
"Lovie I have plans with the guys today" and soon the truth is in sight

Love is a false concept, a repeating dream in a dreamer's hopeful mind
Situations that affect those dreams constantly change over time
Love is a cruel mistress who has her way with your mind, soul, and heart
And the pain is a surprise that you can not control without falling apart

YOU HAVE BEEN HERE BEFORE

So you call your sister, or maybe your best friend on the telephone
You let her know that once again you'll be spending the night alone
The tears continue to spill, from both sides as the conversation goes on
Meanwhile, he's out living, dancing with a new woman to the same old song

The morning brings sunshine's warmth and the sounds of birds chatter
You hear the door open and close and think "What does it matter?"
The same ol' lies mixed with an unfamiliar scent of strong perfume lingers
You answer his good morning dear, by giving him the middle finger

You stand alone in the dark chamber, You have been here before
Your mind is racing and so is your heart as you tally up the score
A smoke-stained barely lit lightbulb swinging softly in the stale air
Brings back memories of a time when you thought she still cared

YOU HAVE BEEN HERE BEFORE

Her soul shined with happiness and her smile radiated through her face
These days it's filled with hate mixed in with total disgrace

The snide remarks start as soon as I arrive home from work
And I despise it when you use those words to cause me so much hurt
So when I leave the job not wanting to go home and fight with you again
I stop at the watering hole and pay attention to a woman needing sin

As I hold her tight and whisper those not so innocent lies close to her ear
I remember the time I was whispering these things to you, my dear
I don't know if it was something I did or something that I had said
But I do know we both think this love is now and forever dead
You say goodbye dick, and I say so long you beautiful whore
We are standing together in this dark chamber knowing we have been here before

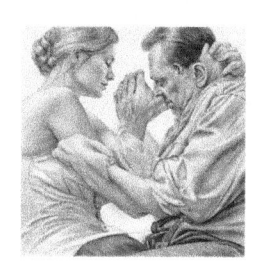

MY TURN TODAY

She gives me unavoidable feelings
The gears in my head start to tumble
I'm feeling heat flow from down under
It's my turn today

I feel like a child, all giddy inside
I want to follow her around all-day
Loving the scenery that I see
Listening to her heels click as she struts
It's my turn today

My words usually rhyme when I put them down
But this feeling has me dazed and confused
A slow strip tease flashes through my mind
And when she turns around I find you
It's our turn today

DREAMS OF YOU

I woke up in a roaring bed of fire
Soaked in the sweet stench of the devil's desire
My mind in a whirlwind of lust and greed
Sexual satisfaction is what this man needs

Things that used to turn me on bring turmoil and pain
What was once sunshine is now thunder and rain
As time marches on my body shows its progression with age
But the fire below still burns with an intense rage

No longer concerned about being in it to win
I'm happy with satisfaction involving any mortal sin
There has to be a way to keep moving ahead
I need hot sex so climb on up into my bed

Until then the showers will be long and cold
Those times thinking of you has to be put on hold
Your hair up in pigtails turns me on
Simple days of friendship are now lustfully gone

Whispering hot breaths of nothing into your ear
Anticipations of orgasms when you draw near
Not another cold shower will I endure
So listen honey, climb up on here

TEMPTATION

Temptation is calling my lonely mind again
Watching the backside of another beautiful sin
She haunts my dreams and waking moments too
Temptation is calling, what am I supposed to do?

The truth is sadder than what I want it to be
The truth be told, she probably doesn't think of me
It hurts my heart to know she doesn't have a clue
Temptation is calling, why am I such a fool?

My mind tells me I know better than to let it be known
It will only bring destruction if my feelings are shown
I'll hide my intentions and let this lust fade away
She will never know how much I'm hurting today

Yes, the temptation is calling my lonely mind again
You are my inspiration for a love that cannot win
If I could only open up and tell you how I feel
Would you understand and could you believe it is real?

Would you just laugh and say I was the fool
Not thinking this hot love for you will never cool
Temptation is calling, and it usually wins the game
Turn around woman and seductively whisper my name

LITTLE SEXY

Little sexy, the tears are falling from my eyes
Little Mama, why are you acting like I am not alive

What else can I tell you?
How can I show you
What can I do to make you realize?

I feel that I need you
I know that I want you
These feelings I continue to hide
Someday maybe the courage will come to me

To fight for this love and then you will see
Until then little sexy, I will remain all alone
And these tears will flow free
When I look into your hazel eyes
Knowing my love for you, you will never see

UNBRAVE BRAVE

Indian squaw, your beauty has shined throughout fifty moons
You're still looking damn good in the high sun of noon
Peace was planted in your soul when you were so young
The dream catcher protected you so no harm could be done

You've danced under the stars and watched the animals roam free
When the cowboy passed by, did you even notice me?
I've smoked peace pipes on the same trail you are now on
Blood has been shed over what someone did or something went wrong

In the warm campfire light, your beauty has shone
With little Chief there we could never be alone
If the stage is set and I'm at the end of my journey
Forget me not and leave your mind without worry

Sitting on the res, waiting for the white man's gold
The medicine man told me I would never grow old
Spent most of my life under the firewater's lustful sin
Now waiting for Mother Earth to open up and let me in

MAGICAL FLOWER POWER

A rose is a flower of magic, a smell good aphrodisiac
Given as a source of affection to reflect undying love
The color of these lush petals is what defines the moment
Providing feelings of joy in the heart from up above

A Red rose shows the passion of the heart and true devotion
While it's a sister of the white variety brings purity and gratitude
Loyalty can be secured with the gift of yellow petals
And after an argument can mellow any attitudes

The rose has been a leader of love through countless ages
A symbol of undying devotion to promise the moon and stars
Smiles light up the room when ladies see them come through the door
They have worked in business and bars to provide happiness for affairs

But the rose is a trickster, a double-edged sword of pleasure and pain
The smell and touch are pure ecstasy pleasuring the very soul
But be careful when handling the emotions of the soul and the heart
Because in love as with the rose, the thorns will in your heart rip a hole

STEP INTO THE DARKNESS

You're sitting there woman, feeling so all alone
You think he is out cheating because he is not at home
Thoughts are caressing your overworked mind
You're sitting at this bar, batting your eyes at mine

Don't hesitate, woman, speak the truth to me
Let's not play games, tell your friends to let us be
Step into the dark side to see what you will find
Lonely hearts like ours get stepped on all the time

Been married so long, you are not sure what to do
You need satisfaction deep inside of you
Your girlfriends tell you that it shouldn't be done
But you desire it, so honey let me be the one

If you speak the truth then you will surely see
We don't have to play games, I can satisfy your wants and needs
Step into the darkness and hold on tight to me
Get ready for the lost sensation of bliss and ecstasy

STEP INTO THE DARKNESS

Waking up in the morning, guilt will soon seep in
You will be overwhelmed with guilt and sin
No confessions to him, you'll let the memory hide
But the anger will continue to build up deep inside

There is always someone as lonely as we are now
Stepping into the dark side can cure that itch somehow
People can call this a mortal sin if they so choose
Being lonely in the night is a feeling we can afford to lose

DOUBLE DOWN

A mystical elf appeared before you on this day
Said he had a game that only two could play
He swore you would like it because no one could lose
He covered you in magical dust to get you in the groove

Warmth spread through your body as he massaged your toes
Soon you were moaning oh God and Oh nos
Cherry-scented oil was rubbed into your skin
You started thinking this was a game you could win

He moved from your toes up to the back of your knees
He knew what you liked when I heard you say pretty please
A small incantation was whispered low
You were rolled over gently and slow

The next couple of hours went by in a mutual bliss
As ecstasy filled you with every hot slow kiss
Goosebumps galore arose and skin covered in glistening sweat
That's when I asked if you wanted to up the bet

A smile of seduction accompanied a whisper so soft
You dared me to give you all that I've got
More magical potions were brewed that night
Multiple orgasms made your head feel so light

DOUBLE DOWN

So many positions you said that you had never tried
We went through the night with nothing to hide
Into the dawn, you screamed out with lustful delight
"Want to double down and do it again tonight?"

FADE AWAY

I have these hurting feelings I wish would go away
They just keep getting stronger every day
My heart is aching, as it deals with the pain
I have to keep them buried and it's driving me insane

I tell her that I love her but she doesn't understand
I can not explain to her what was not planned
Maybe when I leave this world I can finally be at ease
But until then, forbidden love fade away pretty please

I can't deal with being around your sensuous beauty
So fade away my unnamed beauty

"TWO MULES"

Your new mule is kicking, he thinks he's pretty tough
But this ol' mule thinks I've had quite enough
I'm going to teach him a lesson, think I'll make him cry
So pack your bags, lady, I don't want any alibis

Call your new lover baby, and tell him that I'm not home
You need him to come over because you feel so all alone
Make amends to me woman, do what I'm asking of you
Let's finish up with him and we can start brand new

Our love was rock solid once upon a time
When I gazed into your eyes I always lost my mind
I loved to go walking, passing time hand in hand
Our hearts beating as one with sunshine blessing love's plan

Times were sweet like honey from the hive of the honey bees
That's why I find it so hard to believe that you're doing this to me
Is he really special or is he just something to do?
Are you out for fun or just wanting to make me blue?

You've got to quit him pretty baby, I can't take it anymore
Tell that mule goodbye honey, and then just shut the door
Push is coming to shove and my hammer is pulled back
Say goodbye to your two mules, baby, as it all fades to black

BAD ASS ALICE

Alice became a popular woman over time
Now another tribute comes forth in a rhyme
Heard of her eating mushrooms back in my teens
Elton told about her in other women's dreams

She made it to TV with her name as the title
So yes, Alice has been around a little while
Was the name "Alice in Chains" a tribute to she
When I'm tripping it's a vivid vision that I see

Never have I met the woman of my dreams
False impersonations represent it always seems
One more day I face the rise of a coming Dawn
But in my head, I hear a different song

Meatloaf singing Two Out Of Three Ain't Bad
Sounds more like the relationships I've had
Continuing the search through this endless human void
I'll look for a "Dirty Woman" just like Pink Floyd

RUNNING FOR MY LIFE

There's a stout oak tree in the valley, a noose hanging from the limb
It will hold my neck today if I don't stay ahead of them
The posse is hot on my trail, they are not slowing down
Because I shot a man in some faraway town

He gave me the wrong answer when I asked if he knew you
Now I'm running for my life, because of something I had to do
No time to stop for some water, Although a drink would be nice
I know when I slow down I'm going to lose my life

Say a prayer for me, to put some distance between them and me
I don't want to hang from that damned old oak tree
The hangman is grinning as he waits to do his job
Your daddy's the lawman and knows he is doing wrong

The man that hurt you now lies in his cold grave
The man who loves you is being chased away
I will keep running, running into the night
And pray that the noose never gets the chance to pull tight

TOLD BY ME

A rhyme that should be told by me regarding what?
Don't jump the gun and tell me to shut up
Read a little more to see where this is going to end
When I finish will it make us foes or friends?

A day starts when the sun tries to rise in the east
Will it provide starvation for words or a royal feast?
Could it be told without gnomes or beautiful fairies
In the end, altered versions provide pits like cherries

Only one end will be provided to you on this day
Make your own ending if you disagree with my way
Words that rhyme dance a jig in my uneasy mind
Sometimes they are off while other days right on time

Today is a day for you to decide on this topic
Is this a cold book or warmer like the tropics?
Do my altered thoughts leave you feeling unease?
Please don't be butt hurt as I write this little tease

Enjoy life my friends each day you have left
Don't lock your mind trying to prevent thought theft
Negativity has its place in every day of life's process
Sometimes it helps while other times it leaves you in a mess

TOLD BY ME

Whereas positive thoughts make your heart beat quicker
Love grows more strongly and bonds are thicker
Friends celebrate joys and we dance in the moonlight beam
And in those cherished moments, life feels like a dream.

'THE FINAL REEL'

Another year has found its way to an end
Filled with mistakes, confusion, sorrow, and sin
This is the last of a long and lonely ride
No more of these will I ever write
There was happiness, tenderness, and new hope
Gave up a thirty-year affair with the booze and the dope
Clarity sometimes opens my eyes to see
There is so much more out there waiting for me
Wastelands I've traveled, on mountains I've stood tall
This new year is bringing me a brand new call
I must turn my back on so many things
To explore what this new decade will bring
Finding new joys that I didn't think could be found
Seeing that my life is being turned around
What lies in store I can only try and guess
Come what may this year I will try my best
Father time keeps on moving, Mother Nature does too
The last of my poems wishing you fair ado
I hope you've understood my words of pain and wit
As I lay down my quill and call this journey of writing quits

I quit writing poetry in 2010 and didn't start again until 2024

EPILOUGE

As I close the final curtain on this book, I leave fragments of my soul laid bare, a testament to the joy and pain involved in the quiet aftermath of passion.

Navigating the Encore

Mystical emotions of the heart leave scars behind
Raging desires of love that are imprinted on our minds
The fire of existence can bring forth pain or joy
And in its wake, we find our true selves, forever intertwined

"May these confessions of desire and passion remind you that we are never alone in our experiences Each poem is a shared whisper, a collective sigh, a universal heartbeat. Thank you for walking this path with me, for feeling these emotions, and hopefully for finding a piece of your own story within these pages".

Ernest Federspiel

ABOUT THE AUTHOR

Ernest Federspiel is a passionate poet and writer who draws inspiration from personal experiences, nature, and the complexities of life's relationships. Through the depths of human emotions, he inks words weaving them around each other to bring you a story from an altered mind.

Connect with Ernest at www.dawgydaddyresponds.org to stay updated on future works and projects.

NEXT UP

SILENT SCREAMS

A View from the Soul's Edge

by
Ernest Federspiel

Prepare to delve into the depths of the altered mind with my second book, Silent Screams, A View from the Soul's Edge. This collection explores another side of the mind's eye, not through love, but by uncovering visions of madness and provoking thoughts through rhyme without reason.

In Silent Screams, A View from the Soul's Edge, you'll journey through a tapestry of emotions, where poems challenge the boundaries of sanity and invite you to ponder the uncharted territories of the *"altered mind"*

.
Release Date: Look for it coming in April of 2025.

SILENT SCREAMS PREVIEW

TIS' THE SEASON

I prayed for mercy to be placed upon my soul
As I placed you into your last chokehold
The pressure was applied and you were losing breath
Your lungs were gasping for something fresh

Tis the season for the lies to come to an end

As your lips turned a duller shade of blue
Our eyes locked and you realized that it was true
When I said that you would die a frightening death
On the day you decided to put my patience to the test

Tis the season to weep for another friend

Your body cooled down as you prepared to depart
My hands relaxed and I reached to check your heart
The beat was slow, faint, and barely coming through
The day of the dead was here and coming just for you

Tis the season to say goodbye again.